W9-BRY-337

Fibblestax

BY DEVIN SCILLIAN
ILLUSTRATED BY KATHRYN DARNELL

Sleeping Bear Press

I dreamed again of Fibblestax,
sitting among his books,

Peering into the candlelight with a calm,
thoughtful look.

For he's the one who gives a name
to every single thing.

If not for him we couldn't talk.
Or read, or write, or sing.

He called the dog a dog
and he named the cat a cat.

He called the little mouse a mouse
and he called the big mouse a rat.

He decided a whisper sounded like a whisper
and a smile looked like a smile.

He called my parents Mother and Father,
and he called me a child.

To be sure, it wasn't Fibblestax
who always gave the names.

There was before him another man,
who ran away in shame.

His name was Carr, a red-faced man
who sat on a hickory trunk,

And gave terrible names to wonderful things
like toad and snake and skunk.

He thought up all the awful words
in a careless, haughty way,

Words like sphere and xylophone
and others I can't say.

He gave the names to all the things
that seem so boring and bland.

And he made up all the doctor words,
the ones I don't understand.

But worst was the name he gave to the boy
with hair the color of flax.

A sweet young boy with a heart of gold.
And he called him Fibblestax.

If the boy was bothered by his clumsy name,
no one heard him say,

And his sunny smile was always there
as he followed Carr each day.

For Fibblestax was very bright
and one of his favorite games

Was to look at all of Carr's mistakes
and think of better names.

"You know," he said to Carr one day,
who was sitting near the stream,

"This gloobywickus in my cup,
why it looks more like cream.

And these flying creatures,
these hootch-barroos, there must be better words."

Carr just groaned, but Fibblestax said,
"They look to me like birds.

A few more things," the boy went on,
"like trees instead of grunks.

And I much prefer the sound of flowers
to the sound of gunnywunks."

"You think it's easy?" old Carr boomed,
full of empty pride,

"Then try it, little Fibblestax,
and we'll let the people decide!"

And so it was a contest.
The whole town would judge the game.

Each was given a list of five things;
each thing needed a name.

"Ha Ha!" laughed Carr, the old buffoon.
"This list is too hard for you!"

But Fibblestax only smiled and said,
"I'm ready to play. Are you?"

The crowd was quiet and looked at the boy.
How could he be done?

"You see," he said, "I've thought of these things,
and I've named them, every one."

Carr was shocked, but Carr was sly,
and he smiled and laughed anew.

"Then let it begin this very day
for I have pondered, too."

Old Mayor Brody held up the list.
"Number one!" he called in a cry.

"Name the drops of water that fall
from a cloudy sky."

"Ah, yes," said Carr, "you mean the droog.
It's droog," he tried to explain.

The crowd looked to the little boy who simply said,

"It's rain."

"Rain," sighed the crowd in a whispering hush,
and they nodded and smiled at the sound.

Carr just "Hummmphed." But though he'd lost,
there were still four words to be found.

"The next," said the mayor, looking at the list,
"is item number two.

A name for the crispy little squares
we eat with soup and stew."

Again Carr smiled. "Poonies!" he said,
and raised his arms overhead.

But Fibblestax hated poonies. "Crackers,"
was what he said.

"Crackers!" cried the laughing folk,
applauding all around.

The mayor was clapping his hands, too,
for that's how crackers sound.

The boy went on to name three and four,
the next two on the list.

While old Carr fumbled,
Fibblestax named oranges and the mist.

"There's just one more," said the honorable mayor,
"the hardest of them all.

This will decide who'll give the names
the rest of us will call."

Carr looked at the boy with piercing eyes
and wiped his sweaty brow.

The crowd grew silent. The mayor stood tall,
and finally said, "Here, now.

This is that feeling, that very strange feeling,
a dreamy kind of cheer.

The feeling that makes you feel so good
when a special friend is near."

The people looked at one another;
what a difficult end to the game.

Each of them knew of that wonderful thing,
but it didn't have a name.

"Mister Carr," Mayor Brody said,
"give us your word if you may."

But Carr stood still, as white as snow.
He had nothing to say.

He shook a bit and bit his lip
and finally said in a shout.

"How can I give this thing a name?
I don't know what you're talking about!"

You see, the things that Carr had named
were things he already knew.

But he'd never felt that special way.
It was something he could not do.

"Perhaps," said the mayor, "there is no word."
And he crumpled the list in his glove.

The people shrugged and looked at the ground
when a quiet voice said...

"Love."

"What did you say?" the mayor asked the boy,
a tear filling his eye.

Fibblestax smiled. "It's love," he said,
and the people began to cry.

They hugged and sang into the night,
till the moon fell from view.

And they left for their homes still saying the word,
the very best word they knew.

Old Carr was gone. He felt so lost,
he simply ran away.

Fibblestax turned to the mayor and said,
"Maybe he'll find it someday."

I know this tale so very well.
And yet there's more to know

So in my dream I turn to ask
one thing before I go.

"Your name," I say,
"is Fibblestax, a terrible name for a man.

You deserve a better name.
Change it if you can."

"Oh, no," he says, "I'll not do that.
It's a little reminder for me

To always find the perfect name
for all the things I see.

And yet," he says, "it's what's inside.
A name sometimes distracts.

For everyone's a special soul.
Even one named Fibblestax."

For Corey, Griffin, Quinn, Madison and Christian, my five favorite words.
—D.S.

For Lydia & Raoul.
—K.L.D.

Sleeping Bear Press

Text copyright 2000 Devin Scillian
Illustrations copyright 2000 Kathryn Darnell

Sleeping Bear Press
310 North Main, Ste. 300
Chelsea, MI 48118
www.sleepingbearpress.com

Sleeping Bear Press is an imprint of The Gale Group, Inc.,
a division of Thomson Learning, Inc.

Printed in Canada
10 9 8 7 6 5 4 3 2 1

Library of Congress Cataloging-in-Publication Data
Scillian, Devin.
Fibblestax / by Devin Scillian ; illustrated by Kathryn Darnell.
p. cm.
Summary: A young boy with the knack for coming up with fitting names for things competes with the imperious man who has been assigning absurd names to see who will have the right to decide what things will be called.

ISBN 1-886947-90-2 (trade)
ISBN 1-58536-165-8 (pbk)

[1. Names--Fiction. 2. Stories in rhyme.] I. Darnell, Kathryn, ill II. Title.

PZ8.3.S3953 Fi 2000
[Fic]--dc21   00-025959